In Noah's memory, Pigface had never been anything other than Pigface.

It was simply the perfect name for him. He was round and plump and pink, with small, red-rimmed eyes behind thick glasses, and a turned-up nose . . .

A gripping and sensitive story about name-calling and bullying at school.

D1386181

www.kidsatrandomhouse.co.uk

YOUNG CORGI BOOK

Young Corgi books are perfect when you are looking for great books to read on your own. They are full of exciting stories and entertaining pictures. There are funny books, scary books, spine-tingling stories and mysterious ones. Whatever your interests you'll find something in Young Corgi to suit you: from families to football, from animals to ghosts. The books are written by some of the most famous and popular of today's children's authors, and by some of the best new talents, too.

Whether you read one chapter a night, or devour the whole book in one sitting, you'll love Young Corgi books. The more you read, the more you'll want to read!

Other Young Corgi books to get your teeth into
Black Queen by Michael Morpurgo
Sink or Swim by Ghillian Potts
The Shrimp by Emily Smith

For more information on Catherine Robinson
visit www.catherinerobinsonbooks.com

PIGFACE

PIGFACE
A YOUNG CORGI BOOK 0552 54860 X

Published in Great Britain by Corgi Books,
an imprint of Random House Children's Books

This edition published 2002

1 3 5 7 9 10 8 6 4 2

Corgi Books are published by Random House Children's Books,
61-63 Uxbridge Road, London W5 5SA
a division of The Random House Group Ltd,
in Australia by Random House Australia (Pty) Ltd,
20 Alfred Street, Milsons Point, Sydney, NSW 2061, Australia,
in New Zealand by Random House New Zealand Ltd,
18 Poland Road, Glenfield, Auckland 10, New Zealand,
and in South Africa by Random House (Pty) Ltd,
Endulini, 5A Jubliee Road, Parktown 2193, South Africa

THE RANDOM HOUSE GROUP Limited Reg. No. 954009

A CIP catalogue record for this book is available from the British Library.

Typeset in 16/20 pt Bembo by SX Composing DTP, Rayleigh, Essex
Printed and bound in Great Britain by
Cox & Wyman Ltd, Reading, Berkshire

Pigface

Catherine Robinson

Illustrated by Sam Hearn

Chapter One

He had been called Pigface for so long,
nobody could remember how or when
it began. A couple of the children in
Noah's class claimed to have started it,
years ago, but Noah doubted it. In
Noah's memory, Pigface had never
been anything other than Pigface.

It was simply the perfect name for
him. He was round and plump and pink,
with small, red-rimmed eyes behind
thick glasses, and a turned-up nose.

But quite apart from the way he looked, the best reason for calling him Pigface – the icing on the cake, as their teacher Mrs Gentleshaw would probably say – was where he lived. Because his father was a farmer, and his home was on a farm; not just any old farm, but a pig farm. So what else could he be but Pigface?

Not everyone called him that, of course. His real name was Albert Percival Harrison (Noah had seen it once, on the register) but nobody called him *that*, either. Noah often thought his own name rather stupid, but if his parents had christened him Albert Percival he reckoned he might have run away from home. The teachers called Pigface "Harry", as in Harry Harrison, but Noah didn't know where that came from, either. He certainly couldn't remember Pigface ever saying "Call me Harry" to anyone – kids or teachers.

Sometimes the teachers told them off, mildly, for calling him Pigface. But most of the time nothing was said. And Pigface himself never complained about his nickname, so they assumed he didn't mind. What else were they to think, after all?

Noah's mum, however, thought differently.

"Just who is this Pigface?" she asked one day, after Noah's friend Jack had been round after school. It was a Tuesday, a PE day, and Noah and Jack had been discussing Pigface's performance in the gym that afternoon.

He had tried without much success to climb a rope, and had got stuck half-way up. He had dangled there helplessly as the rope twirled lazily round, open-mouthed and wheezing slightly with the effort, until Mr Carstairs had been forced to go up the adjacent rope, pluck him off, and descend with him tucked under his arm.

Noah and Jack laughed heartily at the memory until tears of mirth rolled down their faces.

"Is Pigface funny?" Mum asked.

"Funny?" Noah frowned. "Not specially. He's just Pigface."

"You and Jack seemed to think he was pretty amusing," Mum said. "I thought he must be great fun to have you both in such stitches."

"He does funny things, I suppose," Noah told her, "but not on purpose."

"I see. And why do you call him Pigface?" Mum asked.

"I don't know," he said. "I can't remember the reason. It's just his nickname."

"I see," said Mum again. She looked thoughtful. "Do you remember how much you hated being teased when you first started school? You know, when they made fun of your name?"

"That was different. Pigface doesn't mind," Noah declared, pretty sure he was right but not really caring one way or the other. "He likes it."

"As long as you're sure," Mum said. "After all, think how you would feel if it was you."

Of course Noah was sure. Pigface had never said he didn't like his nickname, and surely he would say so if it upset him, wouldn't he? But he never *did* get upset – that was the whole point. Never. Not even that afternoon, after the whole sniggering class had seen him carried down from the rope. He just stood there helplessly on the blue gym mat, blinking slightly behind his specs and looking bemused. Not upset at all.

And as for how Noah would feel if it were him – the very idea was crazy. He and Pigface couldn't be more different, in every way. Noah was tall

and lean, good at games and popular.
When the football sides were picked
during games lessons Noah was usually
one of the captains, and when he
wasn't, he was always the first to be
chosen. Unlike Pigface, whom nobody
wanted and who was always left over
at the end, his fat thighs mottled and
wobbling with cold inside his flapping,
oversized black shorts.

He was just a joke, a big fat hopeless joke. But Mum had never met him, so how could she possibly understand? Noah decided it would probably be best to keep quiet on the subject of Pigface in future.

Chapter Two

The next day Mr Carstairs stood up in assembly to make an announcement. "This is the Under-Eleven team," he said in his loud games-teacher voice that carried right to the back of the hall without any effort at all, "chosen to play in the match against Forest Park next Wednesday."

The small knot of children sitting near Noah stirred a little with excitement and turned to look at him, and Jack dug him in the ribs with his elbow. "You," he whispered, out of the side of his mouth. "Bet you'll be in it!"

"William Jenkins . . ." Mr Carstairs read out . . . "Noah Barton."

Yes! Noah clenched his fist in jubilation. He was so pleased he almost stretched his arm right up to punch the air with triumph, but just stopped himself. It wasn't really a very sensible thing to do in the middle of assembly.

"You're in the team," said Jack afterwards, admiringly. "Cool!"

Noah made an aw-shucks-it-was-nothing kind of face, but he was delighted. He was the youngest by far; everybody else was at least a year older than him.

At lunchtime Danny Gibbs invited Noah for a kick-about in the playground. He was the Under-11s captain, a large, healthy-looking boy with a ruddy complexion and hair the exact colour and texture of straw. Noah was secretly a little afraid of him: he was skilled and fearless on the football field, but off it Noah knew he could be a bully. He'd seen him with younger kids, throwing his weight around, making them get out of his way just because he was bigger than them.

"Want to play with my new Game Boy?" Jack asked Noah after lunch.

Noah shook his head. "Can't. Gibbsy's asked me to play football."

"Do you have to?"

Did he have to! Of course he had to – you didn't turn the captain down, not when you'd only just made it in to the team! Especially not, Noah reflected, when the captain was Danny Gibbs. "'Course I do. Tell you what, though – you can come and watch, if you like."

Jack made a face. "Maybe," he said.

"I'll come and watch," said another voice.

Noah and Jack both turned. Pigface stood there behind them in the doorway, his pale-blue eyes faintly watery behind his glasses.

18

"You?" Noah couldn't hide the sneer in his voice. "What do you want to watch for? You're not interested in football!"

Just then Danny Gibbs came roaring past, a ball tucked beneath his arm. "Come on, Barton, or you'll be late! The others are there already. Cor, what's that awful smell? Oh, it's the pig-farm dweller! Out the way, Pigs."

POOH

Pigface obediently let him go by and went to join Jack, who was standing behind the two piles of coats slung on the ground as a makeshift goal.

"I wish I was in the team," he said, gnawing at a loose piece of skin on his thumb.

Jack gave a scornful snort. "Yeah, right. The day you get on the football team is the day we play the Blind School."

Pigface said nothing – he simply carried on nibbling at his thumb. Just at that moment the ball came flying through the air and landed squarely in the centre of his stomach. He made an odd little noise that sounded exactly like "whoompf", folded over in the middle and slid down on to the ground.

It had the most remarkable effect on the football game. Everyone stopped playing and started laughing, clutching each other with glee. Even Jack couldn't stop himself sniggering. It had looked so funny.

Mr Carstairs, who was on duty, came rushing across the playground as if someone had been murdered. "What's going on here?" he demanded. "Who kicked that ball?"

Ha Ha Ha
Ha Ha Ha

"Me, Sir." Danny Gibbs detached himself from the group and slouched over, still smirking. "It was an accident, Sir."

"Oh, right." Mr Carstairs' tone changed when he discovered the Under-11s captain was responsible. He looked down at Pigface. "Come along then, sunshine – let's get you to the medical room." He helped Pigface to his feet and across the playground, laughter from the footballers following them as they went.

"Did you see that!"
"Did you see the way he fell over!"
"Did you see his face!"
But after a while they forgot their amusement and carried on playing.

Noah tackled Will Jenkins successfully and ran off down the playground, the ball at his toes as if glued there. He dodged player after player, making for the coat-heap goal. Jack and the other kids watching cheered him on. "Yeah, Noah! Go for it!"

But as Noah swerved to avoid the very last person blocking his path – Danny Gibbs himself – he seemed to stumble. Perhaps his foot caught on a crumbling bit of tarmac. Maybe he was distracted by the spectators.

At any rate, Noah faltered, then he skidded, and finally he made contact with Danny's outstretched leg and went crashing to the ground.

Jack rushed over to Noah. Danny Gibbs was already there, bending anxiously over him. Kicking the ball into Pigface's stomach and winding him was one thing, but injuring one of his star players was quite another matter.

"Are you all right?" Jack asked his friend, as the others came charging up the playground, alert to the prospect of drama. "What's he done, Gibbsy?"

Noah lay sprawled on the floor, his left leg at an odd angle, his face a curious shade of greyish white.

"You OK mate?" Danny asked him, crouching down beside him.

Noah closed his eyes, and shook his head. "No," he whispered faintly, and licked his lips. "I'm not OK. Get Mr Carstairs. I think I've broken my leg."

Chapter 3

Noah had to stay off school for some time to allow his leg to mend. At first he revelled in the attention that went with being newly invalided. Mum let him lie in heroic style on the sofa, watching daytime TV. She brought him drinks and snacks at regular intervals, along with the strong painkillers the hospital had insisted he take three times a day.

He had visitors, too. Jack came to see him most days. Danny Gibbs came twice. He was pale and worried-looking the first time, but back to his normal swaggering self the second, obviously reassured he hadn't actually killed Noah.

After Noah had been off school for a week or so, Jack brought round a huge bar of chocolate and a get-well card made and signed by the entire class.

"Hi," he said. He indicated the chocolate. "This is from Mrs Gentleshaw. Don't suppose I can have a bit?"

Noah shrugged. "Help yourself."

Jack broke off a large chunk. "You're dead lucky, having all this time off school."

Noah looked down at his leg, the plaster stiff and unyielding, and beginning to fray at the top where he'd been picking at it. He shrugged again. "Yeah. Whatever."

"The Under-Elevens beat Forest Park," Jack told Noah, happily munching. "Three-nil."

"I know. You told me."

"And there's another match next week, against St Aidan's."

"I know. Gibbs told me."

"Did he? When?"

"When he came to see me."

"Gibbs came to see you?" Jack looked impressed. "You never told me."

"Didn't I?" Noah sighed, bored with the topic, and closed his eyes.

"I don't think so. I'd have remembered." Jack swallowed his chocolate with noisy enjoyment and licked his fingers. "Can I have some more?"

Noah shrugged again, folded his arms and settled back against the cushions.

"What's wrong?"

Noah opened his eyes. Jack was looking at him with concern. "Nothing," he said.

"Is your leg hurting?"

"Not specially."

"Don't you like me eating your chocolate?"

"I told you to help yourself, didn't I?"

"Then what's the matter?"

Noah knew he wasn't exactly acting as if he was pleased to see Jack. He could hear the sulky, whining tone in his voice, but he couldn't seem to stop himself. Just what *was* the matter? His leg wasn't hurting much any more, although it itched constantly under the plaster. But it couldn't be just an itchy leg that was making him feel so bad-tempered. He missed seeing his friends, that was the problem. He missed playing football, and he was sick of hearing about how well the team was doing without him. He was sick of sitting around on the sofa day after day. All in all, he was just utterly and completely fed up, and couldn't wait for things to get back to normal.

It wasn't Jack's fault, though. Noah realized it wasn't fair to take it out on him. He made himself smile. "Nothing really. I'm just tired. What's been going on at school, then?"

"Not much. Usual things." Jack popped another square of chocolate into his mouth. "Oh, I almost forgot. There's a new boy in our class."

"Yeah?" Noah brightened slightly. New pupils joining the school part-way through term were unusual, and therefore worthy of interest. "What's his name?"

"Basil Moroney," Jack said, through the chocolate.

Noah snorted with amused disbelief. "Basil Moroney? *Moroney*? What kind of name is that?" he demanded. "I know — we'll have to call him Moron! Moroney the Moron!"

But Jack frowned. "I don't know. He's not like Pigface, you know. He's well cool."

"Never said he wasn't," Noah muttered, stung.

Jack looked thoughtful. "I don't think we ought to start calling him stupid names," he said. "He must feel a bit strange — you know, being new.

He's just moved here from London 'cos of his dad's job. Something to do with the telly. A director, I think Bas said. Or was it a producer?"

"Wow," Noah said, unable to prevent the sarcasm in his voice. Bas already, was it? Not just Basil, but Bas. *Huh!*

"They've got a massive house. It's got seven bedrooms and a swimming pool. And—" Jack lowered his voice, awe-struck – "he's got a brand-new computer: CD re-writer, laser printer, scanner, DVD, web cam – the works."

"Lucky old Bas."

brand new! laser printer! C-D re-writer! DVD player! "web cam!

"But the funny thing is, he's not spoilt at all."

"Course he's not," Noah said, with scorn.

"No, really," Jack insisted. "He's not. He doesn't go round telling everyone about everything he's got."

"So how come you know all about it, then? You suddenly psychic, or something?"

Jack didn't seem to notice Noah was being sarcastic. "It all came out sort of by accident," he explained. "We were all talking about computers at break. He wasn't showing off. Everyone really likes him."

Noah felt a small stab of something unpleasant. It felt like jealousy, but how could it be? He didn't know this Basil Moroney character, so how could he be jealous of him? He hadn't even known of his existence until a few moments ago.

"You'll really like him too. I can't wait for you to come back to school so you can meet him."

Well, I don't especially want to meet him, Noah thought savagely. All of a sudden, the prospect of going back to school didn't seem quite so bright.

Chapter 4

As soon as Noah returned to school –
the moment he walked, or rather
hobbled, into the classroom – he knew
things were different. Something had
changed. Nothing obvious. The
classroom looked exactly the same as
ever, apart from the displays on the
walls. All the tables were in their usual
places. The computer was still there on
the bench, the reading books on the
shelves. Everything in its customary,
familiar place.

Noah leant on his crutches and looked around, testing the air like a dog. Just what was it? He felt unsettled, uneasy, and couldn't put his finger on why.

Just at that moment the bell went, and a small cluster of children entered the room. At their centre was a slim, wiry boy with a clever monkey face. The children closed around him, chattering excitedly, until all Noah could see was the top of his dark shiny head. Just at that moment he turned, as if sensing Noah was watching him, and everyone around him parted and moved aside.

"Hello," he said, and smiled. "You must be Noah. Welcome back. I'm Basil."

Basil Moroney. A small charge went through Noah, a tremor of a feeling that was quite unfamiliar, and he shivered. *The famous Basil. What right has he got to welcome me back? Like he owns the place – and he's only been here himself five minutes!*

And all of a sudden he understood that a strange force had been at work. Whatever it was had changed the atmosphere in the room – the feeling, the balance of power. It was as if the universe had tilted slightly, and the person responsible was this new boy. This Basil creature.

It seemed that the whole class wanted to be with Basil. As soon as he walked into the room, everyone was clamouring for him to sit beside them.

"Does everybody think Basil is wonderful?" Noah asked Jack at break, and then wished he hadn't as Jack started to tell him how clever and intelligent and generally brilliant Basil was, in every way. Jack and Noah were still sitting together as usual, but the way Jack went on about Basil, with such admiration in his voice, made Noah think his friend was only sitting with him out of habit, not because he really wanted to. He could tell who Jack would rather be with.

It was as if Basil had cast a spell over everybody. When the bell went for lunchtime, Noah took longer than usual to get there because of his crutches. He hobbled along in the wake of the rest of the class, watching them surging around

Basil and begging him to sit next to
them at lunch.

"Nice, isn't
he?"
said a little voice
beside Noah.
He turned
on his crutches,
clumsily. It was
Pigface.

"Is he?" Noah said bitterly. "I wouldn't
know."

"Everyone wants to be his friend,"
Pigface said wistfully. "I wish I was
popular like him."

"Yeah, well, if you had a big house
with a swimming pool, and a fancy
computer, you probably would be,"
Noah told him, stomping off on his
crutches. "And a dad who works on
the telly," he added over his shoulder,
"instead of on a pig farm."

Unexpectedly, Pigface turned red.

"Where's Jack?" he asked Noah, hurrying after him.

"Classroom monitor," Noah said shortly. That was something else that had changed while he was away. "He's helping put out all the stuff for Art after lunch."

"Oh yeah." They had reached the end of the lunch queue. "Do you want a hand?" Pigface asked Noah.

Noah looked at the people at the other end of the queue, carrying their trays of food. He looked down at his own hands, resting on the crutches, and realized. There was no way he could walk *and* carry his lunch.

Why hadn't he thought of that? Why hadn't Jack, his supposed friend? He felt stupid; foolish, caught out.

"I don't mind helping you," Pigface said. "Honest."

"OK then." Noah's voice was gruff. "If you want."

Because Pigface had carried his lunch for him, Noah felt he couldn't very well go and sit down somewhere without him. So they sat there together in silence and ate their lunches, and Noah ignored Pigface, watched his friends clustering around Basil and wondered just what was so special about him.

After lunch Mrs Gentleshaw came up to Noah in the art lesson. They had all been told to paint something to do with the sea, and everybody was milling around, choosing their paints and spreading paper on their tables, with a great deal of chatter.

"Is everything all right?" the teacher asked Noah.

"Yes, thank you," said Noah, puzzled. Why shouldn't everything be all right?

"I was wondering if your leg was hurting," she went on.

Noah looked down at his leg. It hadn't hurt for ages now, weeks. It was just a nuisance still having to use the crutches.

"It's fine," he told Mrs Gentleshaw.

"It's just that you seem a bit quiet."

Noah wondered why she was bothered. What did she expect him to be doing, jumping from table to table and entertaining the class with funny faces and jokes? Besides, he could hardly get a word in edgeways with Basil hogging all the limelight. Who wanted to speak to him now the famous Basil Moroney was around?

He could hardly say all that, though.

"I'm fine," he said again instead, and got down to his painting with a severe do-not-disturb expression on his face.

Jack turned to him during the lesson, holding a paintbrush loaded with cobalt blue. "Are you all right?" he asked.

Noah sighed impatiently. "Of course I'm all right."

"I just wondered if your leg . . ."

"My leg's fine, OK?" Noah said shortly, and turned back to his own painting. Why did everyone keep asking if he was all right? Why couldn't they all just leave him alone?

"That's good," said an admiring voice suddenly in Noah's ear.

Noah span round abruptly, or as abruptly as was possible with crutches. "What?"

"Your painting." It was Basil. "It's really good. I'm useless at art."

Noah looked at

Basil's own effort. It was an abstract swirl of brilliant vivid colours, peacock green and magenta and turquoise, and at its heart was a leaping silvery dolphin. It didn't look useless to Noah. Far from it.

"Yeah," he said scornfully. "Whatever," and he turned back to his own work. It was a picture of the beach, sea and sand and sky, and it looked flat and boring even to his own eyes.

"No, really," Basil insisted gravely.

"It's excellent. Honestly."

Noah turned to face him again slowly. "You don't have to be nice to me," he said. "You don't have to say nice things about my picture. You don't have to – to *patronize* me!"

Basil looked taken aback. An expression of pained surprise spread across his features, and he frowned slightly. "I'm not," he said. "I'm not patronizing you."

"Yes you are. You're pretending your picture is rubbish and mine's good, when anyone with half a brain can see it's the other way around!"

Basil looked at Noah, and Noah looked at Basil. Then Basil smiled. "Look," he said reasonably. "I just want to be your friend."

Noah pulled a disbelieving face. "Why? Why do you? You're everybody else's friend – why should you need me, too?"

And he turned away from him, back to his picture, and daubed great black thunderclouds across the sky, which gathered pace and dripped down on to the sea and the sand, and finally covered everything.

Chapter 5

Noah and Jack were still friends. Of course they were. They had known each other for so long. But Noah couldn't help noticing how much time Jack was spending with Basil. It was partly because Noah's bad leg prevented him from going outside to the playground at break times. He was down to using only one crutch now, but he still couldn't get about normally. He couldn't run around at all. And football was out of the question. But it wasn't just in school.

Jack had begun going round to Basil's house too, although he always asked Noah if he minded.

"Do you mind if I go round Basil's tonight?" he would say; or at break, "I'm just going out to have a kick-around with Bas, is that OK?"

Noah wanted to say "No, it's not OK," or "Yes, I do mind." But how could he?

"I haven't seen much of Jack recently," Mum said one day, when Noah got home after school. "Is everything all right between you two?"

"Of course it is," Noah told her. He took two slices of bread out of the bread bin. "Can I make some toast? I'm starving."

Mum reached into the cupboard for the peanut butter. "Why don't you ask him round for tea one day this week?"

"Who?" Noah jammed the bread into the toaster and pushed the handle down.

"Jack, of course!" Mum laughed. "That's who we're talking about, isn't it?"

"Oh yeah."

"So why not ask him? What about Friday? You could get a video, make it a sleepover."

The toast popped up. Noah put one slice on a plate and spread it carefully with peanut butter. He cut it in half, took a bite and chewed it carefully. He swallowed. Then he answered Mum. "No," he said, shaking his head. "I don't think so."

Mum was puzzled. "But why not?"

"I don't think he'd want to come. I think he'd rather be with Basil."

"Who's Basil?"

"New kid." Noah peanut-buttered the second slice of toast thickly and poured himself a glass of milk. "Is it OK if I take this upstairs? I've got homework."

Before long, it seemed to Noah that nobody in the class was talking to him. It wasn't that they were ignoring him, exactly. More that Basil Moroney was so obviously Flavour of the Month, and Noah didn't see how he could possibly compete. Actually, he didn't see why he should even try.

To be strictly truthful, there was somebody who was talking to Noah more and more, and that was Pigface. Every day he sidled up to Noah, in lessons, at break, and stood around chattering to him. Or rather, chattering *at* him. Noah rarely said anything back, but that didn't seem to worry Pigface.

He just prattled on; Pigface, who had barely had a word to say to anybody before now. It was as if he recognized a fellow outcast, another loser like him. Noah was being befriended by Pigface, the class joke! He would have preferred it if nobody at all spoke to him.

"Look at him," Noah said one day during English, looking over at Basil. He was standing at Mrs Gentleshaw's desk, showing her a piece of work. "Look at the teacher's pet!"

"Basil's not a teacher's pet. He's probably only asking her a spelling or something," Jack said.

A tinkle of laughter came floating over from the teacher's desk.

"Oh, yeah," Noah said, in furious disgust. "Sucking up, more like! Just look at him – oh, Miss, look at my wonderful poem, Miss! Don't you think I'm the bee's knees, Miss – don't you think I'm the cat's whiskers, the vicar's bloomin' *knickers*!"

The last word came out louder than Noah had intended. Much louder. There was a small silence. Noah had heard of the expression "He wished the ground would open and swallow him up", but before now he hadn't really understood just what it meant. He did now, though.

"Noah Barton." Mrs Gentleshaw was standing in front of him, looking stern. "Get on with your work, please. In silence. I don't want to hear you shouting out words like that in my classroom again."

A shocked thrill passed through the class like an electric current. Noah knew that it was not because he had shouted "knickers" in Mrs Gentleshaw's classroom, but because he had been so horrible about the saintly Basil Moroney.

No-one's ever going to talk to me again, thought Noah, sunk in gloom and embarrassment. I've really done it, now.

But the worst thing of all, worse even than having only Pigface to talk to, was not being able to play football. He could hobble out to the playground at break times now, and he could see the others running up and down, kicking a ball around. He would stand and watch them enviously, dreaming of the time when his plaster was off, the crutch cast aside. He could join in then, like old times. The good old days, he thought wistfully. They all wanted to be my friend then. They'll all talk to me when I can play football again.

He was watching them one day when the ball landed near his feet, kicked by none other than Danny Gibbs.

"Kick it back," commanded the Under-11s captain, before he realized at whose feet the ball lay. "Oh, it's Noah's Ark. You can't kick any more, can you? Sorry, didn't realize! Go and fetch it, Dud!"

Steven Dudley was Danny Gibbs's best mate, and the team's champion goal scorer. He sprinted over to where Noah stood. Noah bent to retrieve the ball, with some effort, and handed it over.

"Thanks, Noah's Ark." Steven Dudley lobbed it back into the game with practised ease.

Noah felt his face turn crimson with shame and anger and frustration. Nobody had called him Noah's Ark since he'd first started school. The teacher had put a stop to it then, he remembered.

He thought he'd forgotten all about it, but he remembered it now, all right. And remembering it made him feel upset and little and feeble all over again.

Noah watched the players rushing about with energy and enthusiasm and skill. There was Danny Gibbs, and Steven Dudley, and all the others. Even Jack was being allowed to join in today. And there, at their centre, was Basil Moroney.

Noah felt he might choke with the strength of the feelings inside him. He turned away and began hobbling back to the classroom.

"Never mind," said a sympathetic voice beside him. It was Pigface. Of course. "You'll be able to play again soon. I'm sure you will."

"Oh, just shut up!" Noah flung at him furiously, and stumped off as fast as his one good leg could carry him.

The next morning Mr Carstairs stood up in assembly. "This is the Under-Eleven team chosen to play against Ransome House next week," he announced.

Noah felt a flutter of excitement, despite himself, but stopped his ears. What was the point of even listening when he knew his name wouldn't be on the list? Probably never will be again, he thought gloomily.

Mr Carstairs was coming to the end of the names now. "Steven Dudley . . . William Jenkins . . . Basil Moroney."

And Noah's misery was complete.

Chapter 6

Noah's plaster finally came off on a
Friday. The following Tuesday was a PE
day. At last he could join in again. They
were playing softball and, to Noah's
horror, Mr Carstairs paired him and
Pigface together.

"You can help him, Harry," the
teacher told Pigface. "Practise some
gentle throwing and catching together.
Give him a bit of a hand."

"A bit of a trotter," Noah heard someone whisper, and he blushed with shame. To think he'd come to this: him, sporty Noah Barton, youngest-ever Under-11s player, reduced to being helped at pathetic throwing and catching by fat ungainly Pigface!

Halfway through the lessons someone came in with a note for Mr Carstairs. "I've just got to nip out to the office for a moment," he told the class. "Just carry on sensibly, please."

Jack went over to Noah. "Are you all right?" he asked.

"Why wouldn't I be?" Noah snapped.

Jack gave him a strange look, and a small pang went through Noah.

The trouble was, he couldn't seem to stop the boiling feelings bubbling up, or the angry words coming from his lips. It was as if there was a well of poison deep inside him. It wasn't caused by Jack, though. Noah knew that. It was caused by Basil.

"Catch, Noah!"

Pigface lobbed another foam ball clumsily, underhand, and it swung away a metre past Noah's left shoulder. Noah leant awkwardly sideways, stuck out his arm, overbalanced and fell to the floor with a thud. The entire class dissolved in laughter.

"Butterfingers!"

"Oops, dropped it!"

"Noah, Noah!"

"Where's the flood, Noah! Where's your ark!"

Noah picked himself up with dignity. Only his pride had been hurt, but the whole class was laughing at him. Even Jack was sniggering. The only person who wasn't laughing was Pigface.

"Go on," said Noah loudly, getting to his feet and spreading his arms wide, "have a good laugh at me. Ha ha ha!

Go on. It's so funny to laugh at someone for doing something they can't help, isn't it? And as for laughing at their name – well, that's absolutely hilarious."

Most of the laughter stopped, although one or two were still giggling. Pigface opened his mouth as if he was about to say something, but at that moment the door opened and Mr Carstairs came in again and started chivvying them all back to the softball.

"Sorry," Jack said to Noah in the playground at break. "Sorry for laughing at you earlier, when you fell over. You just looked so funny. Did you hurt yourself?"

But before Noah could answer, Rosie Bailey from their class came bouncing over, her plaits flying. She looked full of self-importance. "So, are you coming to the party, Jack?"

"What?" Noah frowned, puzzled. "What party?"

Rosie and her friend Emily giggled behind their hands in a particularly silly way. Out of the corner of his eye Noah could see Jack waving his hands around and shaking his head and mouthing "No!" in a for-goodness'-sake-don't-tell-him kind of way.

hee hee!
hee hee!

Noah glanced at Jack sharply. "What party?" he repeated suspiciously.

The girls giggled again.

"Basil's party," Rosie said. "His birthday party. On Saturday."

"He's invited the whole class," Emily put in smugly. "Except you. And Pigface."

"He doesn't want you to come because you *smell*!"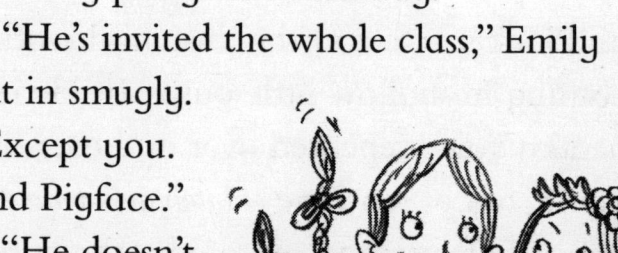

shrieked Rosie triumphantly, and they linked arms and tripped across the playground, laughing loudly.

Noah glared at Jack accusingly, and Jack just shrugged.

It was the shrug that did it. Noah's face contorted with rage, his fists clenched at his sides. Before he knew what he was doing he had launched himself at Jack.

The two boys fell to the ground, Noah punching and kicking at every bit of Jack he could reach, and Jack fighting him back, blow for blow. The blood pounded in Noah's ears as he and Jack scuffled in the dust, his breath coming in shallow little gasps. Inside his head a voice repeated over and over again, full of loathing, *Hatehatehatehate.* He wasn't sure any more who the hate was aimed at. It was just there, inside him, all the time.

Everyone else in the playground clustered excitedly around the two struggling boys. "Fight!" they chanted. "Fight! Fight! Fight!"

Mrs Gentleshaw was on playground duty. Noah was suddenly aware of her legs and feet, looming in front of his face.

He and Jack unfastened themselves reluctantly and scrambled to their feet. They stood before the teacher, hanging their heads in shame and waiting for her to tell them off.

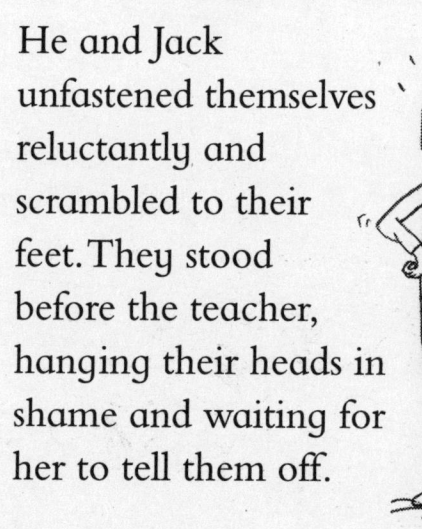

But she never did. When Noah couldn't bear the waiting any longer and risked looking up, he was amazed to see that Mrs Gentleshaw didn't look angry at all. She looked upset and bewildered. She shook her head sadly. "But you're friends," she said at last. "Best friends. Why are you fighting? Best friends don't fight."

And neither Jack nor Noah could answer her.

Chapter 7

"Why?" Mum said. She shook her head
too, sadly, as Mrs Gentleshaw had done.
"Why fight with Jack? For that matter,
why fight at all? It's so unlike you,
Noah. I just don't understand . . ." She
trailed off sadly, as if she didn't know
what to say.

Noah didn't know, either. He had
been expecting her to be angry with
him, but she hadn't been. Just like
Mrs Gentleshaw. In an odd sort of
way Noah wished somebody *would*
be angry with him. You knew where
you were with grown-ups' anger.

But all this bewilderment, this mournful shaking of heads – how was he supposed to respond to that?

At teatime he trudged downstairs to the kitchen, where Mum was ladling baked beans on to a plate of beefburger and chips. His favourite. The smell was wonderful, homely and comforting. Despite his tiredness, Noah's mouth watered and his stomach gave a little gurgle.

"Here's your tea."

Noah sat down and Mum set the plate in front of him. She laid a hand on his head, briefly, and for some reason Noah felt tears well up behind his eyes. There was a big lump in his throat. He swallowed it, along with his mouthful of burger, and dashed at his eyes with the back of his hand.

"Noah," Mum said, looking hard at him. "What's the matter?"

Noah crashed his knife and fork down on the plate. "Why did you call me Noah?" he demanded.

Mum looked taken aback. "What d'you mean?"

"My name!" Noah almost shouted. Why was she being so thick? "Why did you call me Noah? It's a stupid name!"

"No it isn't." Mum spoke calmly. "It's a very old and dignified name. We named you Noah after your great-great-great-uncle, Noah Trevelyan. He was a preacher from Cornwall. He was a very respected and talented man."

Noah was unimpressed. "Bet he was rubbish at football," he muttered.

Mum stood up and picked up Noah's empty plate. "There's trifle for pudding, if you want any. Oh yes, and Mrs Harrison rang."

"Who?" Noah looked blank.

"Mrs Harrison. Your friend Bertie's mum."

"Who's Bertie? I don't know anyone called Bertie." All of a sudden, light dawned. *Bertie*. Bertie Harrison. Albert Percival Harrison. "Oh – you mean *Pigface*!" A suspicious thought crossed his mind. "Why did she ring? Was it to complain?"

"To complain? What would she be complaining about? No, she was ringing to ask you over for tea."

Whatever Noah might have been expecting, it certainly wasn't that. *Tea at the pig farm*, sang a nasty little voice in his head.

"On Saturday," Mum said, and opened the fridge. "She thought it would be nice for you boys to get together. She said Bertie's always talking about you. Noah this, Noah that. Sounds like you've got a fan."

"Mum," Noah said crossly, "It's Pigface."

"Well, I think you should go."

"But I don't want to. Mum," he beseeched, "it's Pigface. *Pigface!*"

Mum looked at him closely, the bowl of trifle in her hand. "She said something about not being invited to a party. Basil Moroney's birthday party?"

She put the trifle on the table. "She said to take your wellies, and you can have a good look round the farm. Have a ride on the tractor, that kind of thing. To make up for missing the party."

Basil's party.

He's invited the whole class. Except you and Pigface. Noah could hear Emily's smug voice now, see Rosie's spiteful face.

"Anyway," Mum went on. "It's too late. I told her you'd love to go. That's OK, isn't it? Now eat your pudding, before it gets warm."

Noah was dreading going to school the next day. He kept thinking Pigface was going to blurt out the fact that Noah was going to tea with him on Saturday. How embarrassing would that be, if people got to hear that Noah hadn't just been befriended by Pigface, but was actually going to the dreaded pig farm! He shuddered at the possibility. But rather to his surprise Pigface said nothing about the invitation, just gave a secret smile whenever their eyes happened to meet.

Mum drove Noah over to the farm shortly after lunch on Saturday. If he had thought about it at all, he had imagined the Harrisons living in some kind of filthy rotting hovel at the end of a pitted muddy track, surrounded by a field or two of rootling pigs, stinking and scabby. He hadn't expected this long tree-lined drive, or the large elegant farmhouse of pale honey-coloured stone.

Pigface appeared round a corner as the car crunched over the gravel by the front door. He was dressed in jeans and wellies, his hair ruffled and his plump cheeks pink from being outside. "Hi!" he said. "You came! Cool!"

Mum opened the door for Noah, leaning across him. "I'll come and pick you up later. Ring when you're ready. Enjoy yourself." Then she whispered in his ear, for him alone to hear. "And be good."

Noah felt cross – what did she have to say that for? She hadn't said that kind of thing to him since he was a little kid.

The annoyance disappeared, though, as Pigface bore him off for a grand tour. Noah was astonished. The farm was enormous: acres and acres of emerald-green fields, criss-crossed with ancient hedgerows and small streams, and dotted everywhere with the pale shapes of the pigs. Odd wooden arcs were placed here and there as shelter for them. There was a large Dutch barn and some low stone outbuildings,

and a grain silo for keeping feed.

The farm wasn't just for pigs, though. There were some cows too, black-and-white Friesians standing about munching contentedly, and in the distance Noah could see two fields of sheep. Pigface spoke knowledgeably about the animals' feeding regimes and breeding seasons and overwintering as they bumped along in a hay-filled trailer towed by the promised tractor.

"Thanks, Sid!" Pigface said to the tractor-driver as they jumped out into the yard. Two black-and-white dogs shot out from the doorway of one of the outbuildings, barking angrily. Noah shrank back. He liked animals on the whole, but he was never totally happy around strange dogs. Especially when they were making as much noise as these two.

Pigface shouted at them and the barking stopped, although the larger of the two continued to bare its teeth at Noah, snarling aggressively.

QUIET!

"That's enough, Kim," Pigface told it sternly. "It's OK," he told Noah. "They won't hurt you. They're just protecting their farm."

"*Their* farm?" Noah noticed the long chains tethering the dogs to the outside of the building, and started to feel a bit safer. "Does your dad know his dogs think it's their farm?"

Pigface laughed. A lot. It was as if Noah had made the funniest joke of all time. It was much nicer when people laughed at things you said on purpose, Noah decided, rather than things you did by accident.

"You lads having fun?" It was Sid. He'd parked the tractor across the other side of the yard.

"Yes thanks," Noah answered politely.

"That's good." Sid turned to Pigface. "You still going to help me change that fan belt on the Land-Rover?"

"I don't know." Pigface looked doubtful. "Not as Noah's come over."

Sid nodded. "You want to hang out with your mate. Fair enough. But I'll be seeing to it in about half an hour, if you still want to lend a hand."

"You don't really know how to change a fan belt, do you?" Noah asked Pigface, watching Sid as he strolled across the yard, whistling.

"No," Pigface admitted. "He was going to show me. But I do know how to clean plugs and points," he added.

"Yeah?" Noah felt a touch of admiration, despite himself.

"Yeah. And I can start a flat battery with jump-leads."

"Cool!" Noah was impressed. He wouldn't even recognize what a jump-lead was, let alone know how to use one.

"And Sid lets me drive the tractor sometimes."

"No way!"

"Yeah, he does. Only for a minute or two, though, up in the field. Where it's safe. Only don't tell my dad – he'd go ballistic if he knew," Pigface said cheerfully. "Come and see the piglets. You'll like them."

He pushed open a low wooden door
and they went in. Noah wasn't sure
what to expect, but it was the best bit so
far: little pink snuffling things, lined up
in neat sausage-like rows against their
mothers' sides, contentedly suckling. They
were not dirty and smelly at all, but
small and clean and perfect.

"Oh!" Noah breathed, leaning over
one of the pens. "They're so *cute!*"

"I saw all those being born. Two weeks ago."

"Did you?" Noah was awestruck. "You actually saw them – coming out? What did they look like?"

Pigface shrugged. "Like piglets being born." He stood up. "Look, I think I'll just go and have a word with Sid. Shan't be long."

Noah stayed with the piglets. They had finished feeding now and were all fast asleep in an untidy pink pile, twitching slightly amongst the straw. One of the sows lumbered to her feet suddenly and began to grunt noisily at him, and he spoke soothingly to her until she lay down again. He looked at his watch. Pigface had been gone for ages. He decided to go and wait outside.

It had been dark in the pigs' shed, and as he emerged into the yard he was dazzled by the sunshine. He lifted his arm to shield his eyes, and it was as if all hell had been let loose.

It wasn't all hell, though. It was the two sheepdogs. Afterwards, when it was all over, it was the suddenness of the dreadful barking that Noah remembered; the barking, the snarling and the baring of sharp terrible teeth, and the dreadful realization that the two dogs were no longer tethered to their chains. He truly thought that they were going to leap for his throat and tear it out and kill him, right there on the dirty puddled concrete of the farmyard.

Chapter 8

"Down, Kim! Lie down, Jess!"

The voice came from nowhere, startling Noah just as much as the dogs had. To his immense surprise and relief, the dogs slunk instantly to their bellies. The barking stopped, but they continued to growl threateningly, their top lips curled up to expose the razor-sharp fangs.

"That's enough now! Be quiet!"

It was Pigface, hurrying across the yard towards Noah, looking anxious. Sid was a few paces behind, and when the dogs saw him they got to their feet and greeted him with wagging tails and lolling tongues. It was hard to recognize them as the savage monsters that had almost frightened Noah to death just moments earlier.

"Are you OK? Sid let them off the chains to take them up to the sheep, but they snuck back here. I was just coming round the corner after them – I saw you standing outside the shed and putting your arm up. I think you startled them. I know they make a lot of noise but they wouldn't have hurt you, honestly. They were just protecting the farm."

Noah looked at them, frisking round Sid like puppies, and swallowed. He was still trembling, his knees weak and wobbly, as if he'd just stepped off a rollercoaster.

"I'm sorry." Pigface touched Noah on the arm shyly. "You must have been scared."

No I wasn't. The words were in Noah's mouth, ready to say. He looked up into Pigface's worried pale-blue eyes and he had the oddest feeling. It was as if it was the first time he had ever seen him – properly looked at him.

"Yes," said Noah instead. "I was."

Sid came over, the two dogs still playing around his heels. "You all right, lad?" He looked concerned. "It was my fault, I should've been keeping a proper eye on them. They know the sows are in there, see, and their babies. They must have just seen you outside, and, well . . ."

"I know," Noah said. "They were protecting them. Pig – er, Harry explained."

"Did he, now." Sid looked at Pigface. "Well, he's right. And he knew what to do. They'll always lie down on command – they're properly trained, see. Matter of fact, they'd most probably have lain down if *you'd* shouted at them to. They're good dogs really. But you weren't to know that. It must have been a shock for you."

"It was a bit. But I'm OK now." Feeling braver, Noah put out a tentative hand and stroked a black head, shining silkily in the sunlight. The dog put out a pink tongue and licked his wrist, once, as if to show there were no hard feelings.

After Sid had gone, taking Kim and Jess with him, Pigface apologized again.

"You don't need to keep saying sorry," Noah told him. "It wasn't your fault. Sid said so. Anyway, you saved me, didn't you?"

"Did I?"

"Course you did. You called them off me. You shouted at them to lie down."

"I s'pose, but . . ." Pigface shrugged. "I wanted you to have a nice time today. I wanted *us* to have a nice time."

"I have had a nice time."

"Honest?" Pigface's eyes widened in surprise.

"Honest. Even though the Killer Dogs from Hell nearly got me."

Pigface smiled. "Yeah, right. So d'you want to come back sometime, then?"

"Don't see why not," Noah said. "If you want me to. But on one condition."

"What's that?"

"That you tell Kim and Jess first."

Pigface smiled again. "OK. But I've got a condition too."

"What condition?" Noah was surprised. Pigface accepted things; he didn't make demands.

"That you call me Harry. It's what you called me just now, to Sid. It's what everybody round here calls me — well, everybody except Mum. She calls me Bertie."

And you lot, who call me Pigface. Noah could see the words floating above his head, as clearly as a thought-bubble in a comic. It was quite a shock. He had been called Pigface for so long, and everyone had just assumed he didn't mind. Then another thought popped suddenly into Noah's mind. *Noah's Ark,* he thought. *You minded that, didn't you?*

The two boys regarded each other solemnly, and Pigface stuck out his hand. "Deal?"

"Deal," Noah replied, and shook it.

They went and found Sid, and he
showed them both how to change the
fan belt and then let Noah top up the
oil in the engine and check the level
with the dipstick.

Then it was time for tea, back in the
farmhouse. It was burgers and chips.

Noah's eyes lit up when he saw it.
"Yum," he said. "My favourite."

"Is it, lovey?" Mrs Harrison was kind,
with a sunny smiling face. "That was a

good guess then, wasn't it? So what d'you think of our farm? Haven't been bored, I hope."

Noah speared a chip. "No," he said truthfully. He thought he wouldn't mention the incident with the dogs. "I haven't been a bit bored. I think it's a great farm."

"Bertie always seems to enjoy himself here." She looked at her son fondly. "He hasn't got his own computer, or a telly in his bedroom. But he always says he's quite happy just pottering around."

"I am," he protested. "I'm going to take over here when I'm grown up. I'm going to be a farmer too, like Dad."

"Well," said Noah. "I think he's lucky, living here. Really lucky."

And he was surprised to discover that he meant every word.

Chapter 9

"It wasn't the whole class at Basil's party, you know," Jack told Noah on Monday morning, back at school. "It was only me and Rosie and Emily, and a couple of others. Six altogether. Seven, including Bas. It wasn't even that good. His mum made us play stupid games, like we were babies."

"Oh," said Noah. He really couldn't have cared less about Basil's party. The realization made him feel good inside.

"So what did you do, then?" Jack asked. "Over the weekend?"

Noah considered lying. But what was the point? He'd enjoyed himself at the farm. In fact, he'd almost certainly had a better time than Jack had at Basil's party. "I went over to Harry's on Saturday," he said.

Jack stared at him. "Where?"

"To Harry's," Noah repeated. "You know – Pigface. To the farm. To look around, and stuff."

"Oh," said Jack, looking rather stunned.

Noah had thought he'd be embarrassed admitting it, but somewhat to his surprise he wasn't – not at all. Instead he felt quite good about it, as if he was being rather brave and daring.

"Yes," he said, getting into his stride. "In fact, I had a really wicked time."

After lunch Danny Gibbs was organizing another kick-about in the playground. "Jack, you go over there – and Basil, over there!" he commanded, and as usual everyone hurried to obey him.

Noah went over to him. May as well ask, he thought. Can't lose anything by asking. "Can I play?" he asked humbly.

Danny Gibbs turned and looked down at him. He was only a couple of inches taller than Noah, but he managed to make it seem much more. "No," he said. "Push off," and turned back to his self-appointed role of director of operations.

PUSH OFF

Noah stood his ground bravely. "Why not?" he demanded. It was only a playground kick-about, after all: it wasn't exactly England v. Argentina.

Danny Gibbs swung round again, astonished. "Cos I say so," he declared. "And I'm the captain of the Under-Elevens,

and what I say goes. Understand?"

Noah's heart was beating fast, but he was determined not to show Danny he was scared. "Not really," he said, frowning in a puzzled way. "Why can't I play? I'm good at football – you know I am."

"You were," said Danny Gibbs shortly. "You broke your leg. Now you're rubbish. End of story."

"No it isn't," Noah said calmly. "It isn't the end of the story, I mean. I broke it weeks ago. It's better now – look." And he ran on the spot. "See? Good as new."

"What's the hold-up?" It was Basil Moroney, coming over to see why the game hadn't started. "What's going on, Gibbsy?"

"Oh, it's Noah's Ark," said Danny Gibbs, with a dismissive wave of his hand. "Wants to play. Reckons he's up to it now."

"Well, he looks OK to me," said Basil, rather to Noah's surprise. "He was fine in PE the other day. Go on, Gibbsy – let him have a go."

Even more to Noah's surprise, Danny Gibbs gave in. "Oh, go on then," he said grudgingly. "You can mark Bas, as he seems to think you're so good now. Oh – and Noah's Ark – keep up with us, yeah?"

"Yeah, sure. No problem. Oh – and Gibbsy?"

"What?" The Under-11s captain turned once more, impatient to begin.

"Stop calling me Noah's Ark. My name's Noah. Just plain Noah. Yeah?"

And he turned, happily, and ran off to join Basil.

When the bell went to mark the end of the lunch break, Noah and Jack started to head back to the classroom. There was some kind of commotion going on in the far corner of the playground, and as they drew closer they could see Pigface surrounded by a jeering group of three or four older boys from Danny Gibbs's class.

"Yo, Pigface!" Noah heard them say. "Beg for them! Beg!"

The tallest of the boys was holding Pigface's glasses high above his head, waggling them around as they all jeered at him. "Beg! Beg!"

Then the boy with the glasses held
them out in front of him, as if he was
about to drop them on the ground. The
chant turned to "Smash, Smash!" while
Pigface just stood there, half-blind
without his specs, blinking and screwing
his face up and looking small and
scared and defenceless.

Noah was filled with a huge surging
feeling that roared in his head like the
surf buffeting the shore. It drove him
forwards, towards the boys with Pigface
in their midst. "Leave him alone!"
he bellowed.

Jack tried to hold Noah back. "Don't!" he gasped. "They're bigger than you! There's four of them! They'll kill you!"

But Noah carried on, heedless of Jack. So what if there were four of them? Hadn't he just stood up to Danny Gibbs, Under-11s football captain and bully, and won? "They can't take his specs away!" he exclaimed. "He can't see a thing without them! It's just not *fair*! Leave him alone!" he yelled again. "Give him his specs back!"

He felt strong, invincible – capable of anything. There was no doubt in his mind that the boys would do as he said, and sure enough they did. They handed Pigface his glasses and sidled off, muttering; although to be fair Noah suspected it had as much to do with Mr Carstairs, who was on duty, bellowing across the playground at them to get cracking and into class.

"Noah was brilliant," Jack said

afterwards, full of admiration, to anyone who would listen. "He shouted at them to give Pigface his specs back, and they did, just like that! I thought they were going to batter him."

"So did I," Pigface admitted. "I thought he was dead meat."

"I didn't," Noah declared, still full of bravado. "They wouldn't have dared. Not with Sir around."

"It was still brave of you," said Basil unexpectedly. "I was bullied at my last school, and nobody ever stuck up for me."

They all stared at him.

"You were bullied?" said Jack.

'*You*?" said Noah, in amazement.

"Yup," said Basil. "Me."

"But why?"

Basil shrugged.

"Who knows?
Don't know,
don't care. I just
hope it never
happens again."

"Blimey," said Pigface, in wonderment.

"You," said Noah again.

"Bullied," said Jack.

They all looked at each other slowly,
all four of them.

"Anyway," said Basil, "it's over now."

"Yeah," said Pigface quietly. "But
thanks for sticking up for me, Noah.
Nobody's ever done that before."

"Don't be daft." Noah beamed at
him. Who'd have thought standing up
for someone would have made him feel
so good?

"Look," Basil said suddenly, "why don't you all come over to my place sometime? We can play on the computer – I've got some wicked new games."

"All of us?" said Noah.

"All of you," Basil said firmly. "I want to be friends with you all. I've only ever wanted that. You can't have too many friends, in my opinion."

Noah still wasn't sure about being friends with Basil. But he was clearly trying to make an effort, so perhaps Noah should as well. "OK," he said. "Thanks."

"What about me?" asked Pigface in a very small voice. "Am I invited too?"

Basil looked at him, and then smiled. "Course you are, Pigface. The more the merrier."

Pigface opened his mouth as if to say something, and then closed it again. Noah's eyes met his. All that had happened over the past couple of days passed through his mind, like a video on fast-forward: the farm, the cows and the sheep, and the sows with their piglets. Helping Sid with the Land-Rover and the fan belt. Kim and Jess, barking and snarling at him like mad creatures, and how terrified he'd felt, and then Pigface's calm, masterful voice commanding them to lie down and be quiet.

And then today. Finding the courage to tell Gibbsy not to call him Noah's Ark, and Pigface's specs being held tauntingly out of his reach to the jeers of the older boys, and how terrified *he'd* looked. They had both been afraid, of different things, and they had rescued each other, Noah realized. Helped each other out. Like friends do.

Noah took a deep breath. "Listen," he said. "There's something I want to say. I think we should stop calling him Pigface."

The others looked at him in astonishment.

"Stop calling him Pigface?" Jack said.

"But why?" Basil asked, puzzled. "He's always been Pigface, hasn't he? Doesn't he like it any more?"

Noah turned to Pigface – he was looking at the floor, his face pink. He was too shy and too embarrassed about making a fuss to speak up for himself. So Noah did it for him.

"No," he said, "he doesn't like it. He never has. And I don't blame him. I mean, would *you* want to be called Pigface?"

"So what do we call him, then?" Basil asked.

"I think we should ask him," said Noah. "And I think we should stop talking about him as if he's not here," he added.

"OK," Basil said, nodding reasonably.

"Right," said Jack. "So what would you like us to call you, then?"

The three of them – Basil, Jack and Noah – looked at Pigface expectantly.

"Harry," he said, suddenly raising his eyes from the floor and looking right back at them. "You can call me Harry."

And his eyes met Noah's again and they both smiled, a tiny secretive little smile that only they understood.

THE END